D1125351

Pet Friends Forever

The Pet Store
Pet Show

by Diana G. Gallagher
illustrated by Adriana Isabel Juárez Puglisi

capstone

is published by
Picture Window Books,
A Capstone Imprint
1710 Roe Crest Drive
North Mankato, Minnesota 56003
www.capstonepub.com

Library of Congress Cataloging-in-Publication Data
Gallagher, Diana G., author.

The pet store pet show / by Diana G. Gallagher ; illustrated by Adriana Puglisi.
pages cm. -- (Pet friends forever)

Summary: Mr. J's Pet Haven is losing business to a pet superstore, so he decides to put on
a pet show for the neighborhood, and recruits Kyle and Mia to help.

ISBN 978-1-4795-2177-7 (hardcover) -- ISBN 978-1-4795-3803-4 (pbk.)
-- ISBN 978-1-4795-5233-7 (ebook)

1. Pet shows--Juvenile fiction. 2. Pets--Juvenile fiction. 3. Small business--Juvenile
fiction. 4. Contests--Juvenile fiction. [1. Pet shows--Fiction. 2. Pets--Fiction. 3. Pet shops-
-Fiction. 4. Contests--Fiction.] I. Puglisi, Adriana, illustrator. II. Title.
PZ7.G13543Pe 2014
813.6--dc23
2013028615

Designer: Kristi Carlson
Image Credits: Shutterstock/Kudryashka (pattern)

Printed in the United States of America in Stevens Point, Wisconsin.
042014   008193

TABLE OF CONTENTS

Good News

"I think I have just enough money to buy Rex a new toy and some treats," Kyle said as he and Mia walked to the local pet store Friday afternoon. "He'll be so excited!"

Sometimes dog toys were cheaper at the big chain store, but it didn't matter. He and Mia always went to Mr. J's Pet Haven.

Mia suddenly came to a stop in front of the pet store and pointed in the window. "The gerbils are gone!" she exclaimed. "Where did they go?"

"That's weird," Kyle said. "So is the turtle pool."

Mr. J's window display was usually full of animal cages, pet toys, treats, and weekly specials. But today the window was almost empty.

Mia shot Kyle a worried look, and together they turned and hurried inside. Mr. J wasn't behind the counter like usual.

"Mr. J!" Kyle called as the door closed behind him. "What's going on?"

"I didn't do it!" Jethro, Mr. J's pet parrot, squawked from his perch near the front register.

"Where are you?" Mia called.

"In the Wonderful World of Water Creatures!" Mr. J shouted from the back of the store.

Kyle and Mia walked back to the tropical fish department. The turtle pool was on the floor. A dozen little turtles perched on rocks in the sink. But Mr. J was nowhere to be seen.

"Hello?" Kyle called, looking around the empty store.

"I'm right here," Mr. J said as he walked out of the storage room.

"Why did you take the turtles out of the window?" Mia asked.

"I have to clean the pool," Mr. J explained. "It was so slimy they kept slipping off the rocks!"

Kyle and Mia laughed.

"I clean everything and put fresh straw in the window once a month," Mr. J said. "I'm usually done before the store opens, but I got a late start today."

"Can we help you with anything?" Kyle asked.

"Yes!" Mr. J said. He laughed and rubbed his back. "Buy something. Then I'll have a good excuse to take a break."

"Okay," Mia said brightly. "I need some cat treats for Misty."

Kyle followed Mia and Mr. J to the cat aisle. After Mia found Misty's favorite brand of treats, they headed over to the dog-toy aisle. Kyle picked out a chew toy for Rex.

On the way to the front of the store, he grabbed a box of dog treats. They brought everything to the front counter.

Mr. J started ringing up Kyle's purchases first. "That will be twelve dollars," Mr. J told him.

Kyle frowned. "But the last time I bought this stuff for Rex it was only ten dollars," he said.

"My costs went up, so I had to raise some of my prices," Mr. J explained.

Kyle shook his head. "I don't have enough money," he said sadly. "I only brought ten dollars." He reached up and grabbed the dog treats to go put them back.

Mr. J stopped him. "That's okay, Kyle. Today I'll sell you the treats and the toy for ten dollars. Plus a favor. Deal?"

"Deal!" Kyle said with a big grin. "What's the favor?"

"I want Misty and Rex to enter the First Annual Pet Haven Pet Show next Saturday," Mr. J said. "There will be all sorts of categories, like best trick and most well-behaved pet."

"A pet show!" Mia exclaimed. "What a great idea!"

"I'm glad you think so!" Mr. J said with a laugh. "It's a special thank you for my loyal customers. I'm hoping it'll help bring some new customers into the store, too. So tell all your friends."

"Is it just for people with cats and dogs?" Mia asked.

Mr. J shook his head. "Nope! It can be any type of pet," he told them. "I want to get as many people and pets to enter as possible. Otherwise the first pet show might also be the last."

Kyle frowned. "Why would the first pet show be the last one?" he asked.

Mr. J sighed unhappily. "I'm losing more and more business to the big pet store in town," he explained, shaking his head sadly. "They can sell everything a lot cheaper than I can."

"I know," Kyle said, "but we shop here anyway."

"And I really appreciate that." Mr. J said with a smile. "Most of my customers stick with me. But every time I have to raise prices, I lose someone. I'm worried I won't have any customers left soon. I don't know how long Pet Haven can survive."

"Maybe the pet show will bring people back," Mia said hopefully. "If you had more customers, you'd be okay, right?"

"That's what I'm hoping," Mr. J agreed. "If not, at least it will be a fun way to say goodbye to my loyal friends."

Fun, yes, Kyle thought, *but definitely not goodbye.*

2

And Bad News

When Kyle and Mia got home, they took Rex outside to play in Kyle's backyard. The yellow Lab went crazy with excitement when he saw his new chew toy.

"Come get it, boy!" Kyle called, dangling the toy in the air. Rex raced over and grabbed it in his teeth. He and Kyle played tug-of-war for a few minutes before Kyle finally let go. Rex immediately ran off with his prize.

"At least you can still get Rex's toys at the big pet store," Mia said. "They don't sell cat treats there. At least not the ones Misty likes. She's *really* picky."

Kyle could believe that. Misty didn't seem to like anything or anyone other than Mia. "When did you go there?" he asked.

"Last week with Lacey and her brother," Mia explained. "Tommy had to get food for his snake."

That was okay with Kyle. He'd been to the big store with his mom before. Sometimes she had to buy veterinary supplies that Mr. J didn't sell. And Tommy's ball python ate frozen mice. Mr. J only sold live mice to people who wanted tiny pets.

"If Pet Haven closes, Misty won't get her favorite treats ever again," Mia said.

"Pet Haven is not going to close," Kyle said firmly.

"It might," Mia insisted. "You heard Mr. J."

Kyle's mom suddenly appeared in the back doorway. She'd changed into her regular clothes, but Kyle knew she'd probably just come from her clinic next door. "Why would Mr. J close Pet Haven?" she asked.

"It's not for sure," Kyle said. He and Mia explained about the upcoming pet show and what Mr. J had said about losing business.

"But if it doesn't work, he might still have to close," Kyle said.

"We can't let that happen," Mia said. "We have to do something!"

"It sounds like Mr. J *is* doing something," Dr. Blake said. "He's having the pet show to bring in new business. And it's open to all types of animals. That should help. I bet Mr. and Mrs. Cooper would love to show off Porcupine."

Kyle grinned. He was a big fan of Porcupine, a black-and-white pot-bellied pig his mom helped treat. Whenever someone talked to him, Porcupine grunted like he was having a real conversation.

"Will you tell the Coopers about the pet show?" Mia asked Dr. Blake.

"And let us put a flyer in the clinic?" Kyle asked.

Dr. Blake nodded. "Yes to both ideas!" she said.

"We should hang flyers all over town," Mia said.

"You could put an ad in the newspaper, too," Dr. Blake suggested. "Or on the paper's website."

"That's a great idea!" Mia exclaimed. "Mr. J needs a big crowd."

Kyle crossed his fingers. Getting lots of people to come to the pet show was the best thing he and Mia could do to help Mr. J. Everyone was sure to be impressed when they saw how Mr. J greeted all his customers and their pets by name.

Maybe they'll tell their friends about how friendly he is and what good advice he gives, Kyle thought. Then the new people would see the one thing they couldn't get at the big store: Mr. J's personal touch.

"C'mon, Mia!" Kyle said. He grabbed her hand and pulled her toward the house. "We've got work to do!"

3

The Parking Lot Plan

Kyle, Mia, and Dr. Blake went to see Mr. J the next afternoon.

"Get out! Get out!" Jethro scolded Kyle and Mia when they entered the store. He let out a whistle when he saw Kyle's mom.

"Jethro is just as happy to see you as I am, Dr. Blake!" Mr. J said as he shook Dr. Blake's hand. "What can I do for you folks today?"

"We just need a minute of your time," Dr. Blake said. "The kids told me about the pet show, and I'd like to help."

"Fantastic!" Mr. J exclaimed. "One of my weekend workers can help with the store, but I'll need extra hands at the pet show."

"Where are you going to hold the show?" Dr. Blake asked.

"I was thinking of using the parking lot out back," Mr. J said. "Even if only a few people show up, I'm worried the store won't be big enough."

"The parking lot is kind of scary," Kyle said.

"And it's really dirty back there," Mia added, making a face.

"I park there all the time," Dr. Blake said. "It's not that bad."

"Actually, they might have a point," Mr. J said. "Let's go take a look at it."

The group walked through the store and out the back door to go check out the parking lot. Outside, weeds grew through cracks in the pavement. Tall trees with overhanging branches surrounded the lot. The leaves blocked the sun.

Kyle's mom wrinkled her nose as she looked around. "It *is* a little gloomy, isn't it?" she agreed.

"There's so much shade," Mia said. "And barely any sun."

"Actually, I think there's just enough shade," Mr. J said. "Black pavement gets really hot in the sun. The shade will help keep it cool for the animals' feet."

"An excellent point," Dr. Blake agreed. "I'll be here in case there's an emergency, but I don't want to treat burned puppy paws."

"We'll set up a vet tent!" Mr. J exclaimed, clapping his hands together. "I'll have to print up new flyers that say 'vet on site' so people know."

"Print a hundred," Mia said. "Kyle and I will hang them all over town!"

"A hundred!" Mr. J repeated, looking surprised. "How many people do you think will come?"

"More than a few," Kyle's mom joked.

"I hope I have enough ribbons for everyone!" Mr. J said.

"What kind of ribbons?" Kyle asked.

"I was going to hand out first-place trophies for the best pet in each category," Mr. J explained, "and ribbons to everyone else who participates."

A trophy and a ribbon would look great on my bookcase, Kyle thought. *Rex and I have to start practicing!*

"I don't know if I can afford to buy a hundred ribbons, though," Mr. J said. "I was hoping the pet show would help the store *make* money, not spend it."

"What if you sold food and drinks at the show?" Kyle suggested. "That'd make money. And maybe some of the other stores on the block would be willing to help, too."

"That's a great idea, Kyle," his mom said. "I bet some of the restaurants would donate food. After all, more customers at the pet store will mean better business for the other stores nearby, too."

"You'll have lots of money for ribbons!" Mia said.

"Oh, before I forget," Dr. Blake said, "I was thinking we could invite the mayor, the principal of Bear Valley Elementary, and the Chief Animal Control Officer to be judges at the pet show. I bet they'd be happy to help."

"That's a great idea!" Mr. J said happily. "Let's ask them. If they say yes, we'll have to put that on the flyer, too!"

"Don't worry about a thing, Mr. J," Mia said. "The First Annual Pet Haven Pet Show is going to be huge!"

4

Pet Show Prep

Kyle and Mia spent Sunday evening making flyers for the Pet Haven Pet Show. They made sure to include all the information about the prizes, the judges, and the vet tent. Then they handed the flyers out to their friends during lunch on Monday.

"This looks really cool!" Billy Evans said as he read the flyer. "Can I bring Pete?"

Lacey Ortega laughed. "Of course you can't bring Pete!" she said. "He's a toad!"

"Actually you *can* bring Pete," Kyle told them. "He's a pet, and all pets are welcome at the Pet Haven Pet Show!"

"But the weird ones have to be caged," Mia added.

Billy scowled at Mia. "Pete isn't weird," he said. "And he doesn't have a cage, either. He rides in my pocket."

Kyle frowned. Billy really didn't like it when people insulted his toad. And calling him weird wasn't exactly nice. "Pete might win a blue ribbon for riding in your pocket," he said, trying to distract Billy.

Billy perked up. "There's a prize for pets that ride?" he asked.

"There might be," Kyle said. "I don't think Mr. J has picked all the categories yet, so who knows!"

"My brother's snake, the Great Gorgon, rides around his neck," Lacey said.

Mia shuddered. She wasn't a fan of snakes. "He could be in the contest. As long as Tommy's snake stays on his neck and not mine!" she exclaimed.

"Does anyone want to hang flyers?" Kyle asked. "Or help clean the store before the pet show?"

Several hands immediately shot in the air.

"Great!" Mia said. "Mr. J will love having so much help!"

"Let's meet at the pet store after school," Kyle said. "We can see what he needs us to do."

⌣⌣⌣

Kyle, Mia, and their friends all met at Mr. J's Pet Haven that afternoon. There was a lot to be done. The pet show was less than a week away!

Eva, Logan, Conner, and Ryan didn't have pets, but they took Mr. J's new flyers to post around town. Billy and Lacey stayed to clean up the store with Kyle and Mia.

Mr. J handed out rags and spray bottles of water to the kids. "I'll work on cleaning out the tanks and cages," he told them. "You kids dust and organize the shelves."

Kyle teamed up with Mia, and Billy worked with Lacey. They started at opposite ends of the shelves in the aquarium supply section. Kyle and Mia stacked packages of plastic plants in the aisle and started wiping off the display rack. They'd only been working for a few minutes when Lacey suddenly let out a loud scream.

Mr. J came running over right away. "What happened?" he asked.

"Something bit me!" Lacey hollered. "Something gross and slimy!"

Kyle stood on his tiptoes and saw a big black glob of something stuck to the back of the shelf. "I don't think it bit you," he said. "It looks dead."

"Ewww!" Lacey exclaimed, trying not to gag. "I touched it!"

"It's just a fresh fruit treat," Mr. J said. "They're good for turtles and birds." He used a paper towel to pull the glob out.

"How do you think it got back there?" Kyle asked.

Mr. J shrugged. "Who knows," he said. "I'm just glad that we found it before a customer did."

"Especially a new customer," Mia added.

Kyle, Mia, Billy, and Lacey worked hard for the rest of the afternoon. They didn't find any more rotten treats, but by the time they were done, they were exhausted.

"Thanks for all your hard work this afternoon," Mr. J said. "The store hasn't looked this good since I opened thirty years ago."

Kyle glanced around. Mr. J was right. The Pet Haven did look great. The shelves were all stocked with new supplies. Metal gleamed and glass shined. Everything smelled fresh and clean.

"Now go home and rest," Mr. J said. "You worked hard today."

"Go away!" Jethro called as Kyle and his friends headed for the door. "Pizza!"

"I'm really gonna miss that bird," Billy said.

Everyone will miss Jethro if Mr. J goes out of business, Kyle thought.

But that wouldn't happen if the Pet Haven Pet Show was a success. And that depended on how many people showed up.

5

Ready, Set, Show!

Kyle was ready to go bright and early on Saturday morning. He and Rex sat on the front porch waiting for Mia to come over. The pet show wouldn't start until the afternoon, but his mom had to get there early to set up supplies in her vet tent. As soon as Mia arrived with Misty, they would all drive to the pet store together.

"Sorry I'm late," Mia said as she hurried up. "Misty wasn't in the mood to behave this morning. She was hiding under the couch. It's a good thing she likes that new wind-up mouse, or she'd still be there."

Mia set the cat carrier down on Kyle's front steps, and Rex walked over to investigate. Misty hissed angrily from inside when he sniffed the wire door. Rex quickly retreated to Kyle's side.

Kyle ran his hand over Rex's soft fur. The dog had been washed and groomed before the pet show, so he looked his best.

Mia took a seat next to Kyle on the steps. "Are you nervous?" she asked.

Kyle shrugged. "A little," he said. "Rex still won't hold a treat on his nose. Watch."

Kyle told Rex to sit. Then he put a treat on the end of Rex's nose. The dog immediately looked down. The treat rolled right off the end of his nose and hit the ground. Rex quickly gobbled it up.

"He's supposed to wait until I tell him okay," Kyle explained. "Then he's supposed to flip the treat off his nose and catch it."

"But Rex does other tricks," Mia reminded him.

"Most of the time," Kyle said. "I just hope he does them today. I really want to win a trophy."

"Me, too," Mia said. "But I don't think Mr. J will have a Cranky Cat category."

"Too bad," Kyle said. "Misty would *definitely* win that. She's the crankiest cat ever."

Just then, Dr. Blake walked out. "Ready to go, kids?" she asked.

"Definitely!" Kyle and Mia said.

They all piled into Dr. Blake's van and drove to Mr. J's Pet Haven. "Wow!" Mia exclaimed as they pulled around to the back of the store. "This looks great!"

Mr. J had set up Dr. Blake's vet tent in one corner of the parking lot. A hamburger stand from a local restaurant stood nearby. In the middle of the parking lot, four orange road cones connected with rope formed a show ring. A round table with an umbrella stood at one end of the ring.

Kyle and Mia helped Dr. Blake unload vet supplies from the back of her van and carry them over to the tent. They spread out stethoscopes, bandages, doggy toothbrushes, and other supplies Dr. Blake might need.

An hour later, Mia's dad stopped by to see how things were going. "Is there anything I can help with?" he asked as he walked up.

"Where's Mom?" Mia asked.

Mr. Perez pointed toward the umbrella table. "She just volunteered to be the pet show secretary," he said.

Kyle and Mia left Misty and Rex with Mia's dad and went to see Mia's mom. Mrs. Perez sat at the table with Dr. Blake and Mr. J.

"What does a pet show secretary do?" Mia asked.

"I help fill out entry forms," Mia's mom said. "And I'll make a list of all the winners."

"Don't forget to get addresses and phone numbers," Mr. J reminded her.

"I won't," Mrs. Perez promised. She looked at her watch. "It's almost time to start. Are you kids ready?"

"I think so," Kyle said. He glanced around the parking lot. It looked great, but it was still empty. "I just hope other people show up."

Just then, Mia pointed across the parking lot. "Look!" she said. "There's Lacey and Tommy with the Great Gorgon!"

Mrs. Perez gasped. "A snake!" she exclaimed. "My first pet is a snake?"

"Maybe you should sign Rex and Misty up first," Mr. J suggested with a laugh.

"Good idea," Mia agreed. "But I don't think you'll have a category for Misty. The only tricks she knows are eat, sleep, and attack."

"Enter your cat," Mr. J said. "We'll make a category."

By the time Mrs. Perez had finished signing Rex and Misty up for the pet show, two more people had arrived with their dogs. Soon after, Mr. and Mrs. Cooper showed up with their pot-bellied pig. Billy Evans lined up behind them with his toad in his pocket.

Lacey and her brother, Tommy, walked over to say hello. Tommy's ball python immediately raised his head and flicked his tongue out at Billy.

Billy quickly covered his pocket with his hand. "My toad is not a snake snack!" he exclaimed.

Tommy took a step back. "Don't worry, kid. The Great Gorgon doesn't eat toads."

Billy held up a plastic box with holes in the top. "What about newts?" he asked.

"Nope," Tommy said, shaking his head. "Only frozen mice."

"Do your newts all have names?" Lacey asked.

Billy nodded and started counting the newts. "One, Two, Three, Four, Five, Six, Seven, Eight and . . . where's Nine?" He counted them again. "Oh, there he is. Nine was hiding under Eight."

"Uh-oh, Mom," Mia said. "You're going to need help!"

Fins, Fur, Feathers, and Fun!

By the time Mr. J was ready to start the pet show, dozens of parents, kids, and pets had filled the Pet Haven parking lot.

Mrs. Perez was busy making sure all the pets were registered. She had each of the owners list their animal's talents and quirks on the entry form so the judges could create different categories.

When all the pets were entered, Kyle and Mia headed back over to Dr. Blake's vet tent to pick up Rex and Misty. Then they joined the other contestants who were waiting patiently near the show ring.

"Welcome to the first annual Pet Haven Pet Show!" Mr. J's voice boomed over a loudspeaker. "First of all, I want to thank everyone for coming! Let me introduce our judges for the day: Mayor Crocker; Bear Valley Elementary School's principal, Mrs. Johnson; and Mr. Langley, the Chief Animal Control Officer."

The judges all stood up and waved to the crowd. The contestants and spectators all applauded.

"The winners will be announced at the end of the show," Mr. J continued. "So let's get started with the parade of pets. Dogs first, please. Enter the ring, circle once, and exit!"

Kyle led Rex toward the show-ring entrance and told him to heel. The yellow Lab walked quietly by his side all around the ring.

Most of the dogs behaved, but not all of them. A rat terrier yapped and spun in circles all the way around. A few smaller dogs had to be carried. Two hunting hounds raced around three times before their owners caught them. A large German shepherd jumped up and licked the school principal's face.

"He won't get extra points for kissing up to the judge," Mrs. Johnson joked.

The cats were up next. Most of the owners paraded their cats in their carriers. Misty was wearing a leash and harness, but Mia carried her. Only two cats walked on leashes. They both pounced and batted at bugs.

All the other pets were grouped together. Tommy and Billy walked with their pets on their shoulders. Other owners kept their rodents, reptiles, birds, crickets, and hermit crabs in small cages as they walked around the ring. Two parents rushed to rescue fish that sloshed out of round water bowls.

"Thank you, everyone!" Mr. J said as the last animal left the ring.

"Zip it!" Jethro squawked. The parrot sat on Mr. J's shoulder.

Mr. J laughed. "It seems like Jethro is giving us an introduction to our next category: Pets That Talk," he said.

"This should be good," Kyle whispered to Mia.

Three pets entered the ring — a parakeet, a dog, and Porcupine the pot-bellied pig. The parakeet only knew how to squawk one word: "Birdie!" The dog barked. Porcupine grunted, oinked, nodded, and shook his head when his owner spoke to him. Everyone loved him.

"I knew Porcupine would be a hit," Dr. Blake said. She'd walked over from her vet tent to catch the end of the little pig's performance.

"Have you been busy?" Kyle asked his mother.

Dr. Blake nodded. "Way busier than I expected to be!" she said. "I treated a kitten with ear mites, and I've given *lots* of free check-ups."

"Reptiles are next," Mr. J announced. "With and without legs!"

The audience members all laughed, and Kyle smiled. The Pet Haven Pet Show was a huge success so far. Everyone could clearly see that Mr. J was the nicest, friendliest pet-store owner in town.

Tommy entered the ring with the Great Gorgon wrapped around his arm. Two other kids carried smaller snakes in cages. Mr. Bernard marched into the ring with Charley, his five-foot long iguana.

There were other little lizards and geckos, but none were as big or as green as Charley. A large tortoise and some small turtles completed the category.

The judges gave each animal a chance to do a trick or show off. Tommy and his snake were up first.

"Dance!" Tommy said. He moved his finger from side to side. The Great Gorgon followed the movement of Tommy's finger with his head. It looked like he was moving his head to music only he could hear.

"Beg!" Mr. Bernard told Charley. The iguana stared and bobbed his head. When Mr. Bernard held out a peeled banana, Charley ate it in one gulp.

The next category was Creepy Crawlies. Billy Evans entered his pet toad and all nine of his newts. Another boy entered his ant farm. There were also frogs, bugs, and a jar full of worms.

Next up was a category called Fuzzies and Feathers that Mr. J had created specifically for all the hamsters, guinea pigs, mice, and birds. The fuzzies were judged on their wheel-spinning and stick-chewing abilities as well as appearance.

The birds in the category got points for feather-fluffing, head-bobbing, singing, and chirping. Jethro was the best talker out of all the feathers, but he belonged to Mr. J, so he couldn't enter.

Since most of the pet-show contestants were cats and dogs, Mr. J and the judges made up several categories so the animals could compete in smaller groups.

Mia decided to skip the first several categories: Extra Furry, Pounce-and-Play, and Scratching Post. She decided to enter Misty into Cats That Don't Like Anyone But Their Owners instead.

When it was her turn to perform, Misty yawned and dozed off. Clancy, Megan O'Malley's cat, was the only other entry. He hissed at the judges.

"Now it's time for the dog categories," Mr. J announced. "First up, we have Dog Tricks! Take your positions, pet owners!"

There were eleven entries in the Dog Tricks category. Some of the dogs played dead. Some rolled over. Some shook hands, including Rex. Rex also fetched a ball and caught every treat Kyle tossed in the air. Kyle was pretty sure Rex was in first place, but he had one more trick up his sleeve.

"You can do it, Rex," Kyle said as he balanced a treat on the end of Rex's nose. "Wait . . ."

But instead of holding still, Rex dropped the treat and ate it. The audience started laughing loudly.

Kyle shrugged and took a bow. "If it comes down to trick or treat, Rex always picks the treat," he said with a laugh.

Kyle and Mia hung out with their friends until Mr. J called all the contestants back to the ring. It was time to announce the winners. Everyone held their breath as Mr. J took a piece of paper from the judges and started to read the list of winners.

The Great Gorgon won a blue ribbon for Best Dancing Snake.

Billy Evans won for Best Creepy Critter Collection.

Blue ribbons were awarded for One-Trick Dog and Two-Trick Dog. Rex won a blue ribbon for being a Three-And-A-Half Trick Dog.

The biggest surprise was when Clancy beat out Misty in Cats Who Don't Like Anyone But Their Owners.

"I can't believe Misty lost the Cranky Cat category," Kyle said, shaking his head. "I was sure she had that one in the bag!"

"I can't believe Misty has been so good all day!" Mia said. "Maybe she needs to get out more often."

Mia snuggled close to Misty, and the cat immediately let out an angry hiss. Mia laughed. "Or maybe not."

"And now, the Best in Show trophy goes to —" Mr. J paused. "It's a tie! Porcupine and Charley!"

The crowd cheered happily. Everyone agreed that the Coopers' black-and-white pig and Mr. Bernard's giant green iguana *both* deserved the top prize.

Kyle looked down at Rex. *Maybe next year we'll win Best in Show,* he thought. *If Rex learns to do the treat-on-the-nose trick, that is. And if Mr. J's Pet Haven is still in business.*

Suddenly, Kyle realized something. Everyone had been so busy enjoying the pet show, they hadn't done any shopping. Nobody had bought anything from Mr. J's store. Nobody had even gone inside!

Stop, Look, and Listen

"Everyone's leaving!" Kyle exclaimed as parents, kids, and pets all started walking away.

"Because the pet show is over," Mia said.

"But nobody went into the store," Kyle said. "Mr. J didn't get any new customers."

Mia's eyes grew wide. "Oh, no! You're right! We have to do something!"

"Wait up, everyone!" Kyle shouted. "Don't forget to check out Pet Haven before you go home."

"Mr. J has everything you need," Mia hollered. "And he's the best pet expert in town!"

But nobody paid attention to a couple of kids who were talking too loudly.

Kyle looked around frantically. He saw his mom standing near the vet tent. She was talking to the mayor. *Perfect*, Kyle thought as he rushed over.

"Mr. Mayor!" Kyle called as he ran up. "We need your help!"

"What is it, Kyle?" the mayor asked.

"Mr. J was hoping the pet show would help him get some new customers," Kyle explained, "but nobody even went into the store! And now everyone is going home. You have to do something. Maybe they'll listen to you."

"Everyone listens to the mayor," Mia added.

"I hope you're right about that," the mayor said. He walked over to the judges' table and picked up the microphone. "Everyone, please listen up! Stop right where you are!"

Everyone stopped and turned to look.

"Before you take off, let's all thank Mr. J for giving us a fantastic afternoon," the mayor said. He tucked the microphone under his arm and clapped his hands.

The crowd applauded, too.

"Did everyone have fun?" the mayor asked.

"Yes!" everyone yelled.

"Do you want to do it again next year?" the mayor asked.

"Yes!" the crowd shouted back.

"Then take a minute to visit Mr. J's store," the mayor said. "Look around! Buy something! Give the parrot a cracker! And remember, there won't be a second annual Pet Haven Pet Show if there isn't a Pet Haven."

"I hope this works," Mia whispered to Kyle.

Kyle nodded. He did, too. He was out of ideas.

"The back door is open!" Mr. J shouted.

Almost immediately, everyone in the parking lot turned and headed for the store.

"Uh-oh," Kyle said with a gasp. "Now we've got another problem."

"What do you mean?" Mia asked, looking puzzled. "Mr. J's store is about to be mobbed!"

"Exactly," Kyle said. "Mr. J can't handle all those people alone!"

Business Boom

Kyle and Mia rushed back over to Dr. Blake's vet tent to drop off Misty and Rex. On their way back to the pet store, they caught sight of Billy.

"Billy!" Kyle called. "Do you know where Lacey is? Mr. J needs our help in the store right away."

"Doing what?" Billy asked. "We already finished cleaning the shelves."

"Exactly!" Mia said. "That means we already know where everything is."

"And we'll be able to help if one of Mr. J's new customers can't find something," Kyle added.

Billy looked shocked. "You mean you want me to work?" he said.

"Yes," Mia and Kyle said.

Billy sighed. "Okay, fine," he agreed. "Let's go."

They found Lacey already inside the store. She'd gone with her brother to find fresh bedding for the Great Gorgon's tank.

Mr. J was standing behind the checkout counter. The mayor was busy walking up and down the crowded aisles shaking hands and making everyone feel welcome.

"Let's all cover a section," Kyle suggested. "I'll take dogs."

"I call snakes and lizards!" Billy said.

Lacey chose birds, and Mia headed over to the cat aisle. Tommy volunteered to handle the tropical fish department.

Kyle spent the next hour standing around. He smiled and offered to help, but most of the dog people knew what they wanted and had no trouble finding it. He did help a new dog owner find a teething ring for her new puppy, though.

"Thank you so much," the woman said, gratefully. "Everyone in this store is so nice and helpful!"

Kyle peeked into the next aisle. Mia was fawning over a white kitten.

"Do you think Chloe would look better in a pink or red rhinestone collar?" the kitten's owner asked.

"Pink," Mia said. "Definitely pink."

Kyle grinned, remembering when Mia had bought Misty a sparkly pink collar. It had barely lasted a day before Misty chewed through the fabric and tore the rhinestones off. Then she'd scattered the gems all over the Perez's kitchen.

Just then, Mrs. Cooper walked over to them. She was leading Porcupine behind her on his leash. "Do you happen to know if Mr. J has a pot-bellied pig section?" she asked, glancing around.

Kyle leaned down and scratched Porcupine behind his ears. "What are you looking for?" he asked.

"Oink, oink!" Porcupine squealed as Kyle petted him.

"Apple-and-peanut-butter pig treats," Mr. Cooper said.

"Right this way," Kyle said. He led the Coopers over to the treat display at the front of the store.

Mr. J was just finishing ringing someone up as Kyle approached. Kyle recognized the girl from the Fuzzies and Feathers category. Her guinea pig had won a blue ribbon for coming out of his plastic house first.

Mr. J handed the girl a bag. "I'm sure Freckles will like those chew sticks, Charlotte," he said.

"You know our names!" Charlotte exclaimed. "But we've never even been here before."

"No, but you're here now," Mr. J said with a smile. "And I hope you'll come back."

I bet they will, Kyle thought. *Everyone is figuring out how great Mr. J is!*

"I'm hungry!" Jethro suddenly squawked from his perch near the register.

"Can I feed him, Mom?" a boy asked.

"That's up to Mr. J," the boy's mother told him.

Mr. J smiled. "I suppose Jethro can have one more," he said, handing the boy a cracker. "He's been eating all day!"

"Bad birdie!" Jethro squawked, bobbing his head.

Kyle glanced around at the crowded store. Business was booming. It seemed like everyone in town was eager to buy pet supplies from Pet Haven. The pet show had been a huge success, just like Mia had predicted.

I bet the next Pet Haven Pet Show will be bigger and better, Kyle thought, *especially if I can teach Rex the treat-on-the-nose trick. A four-trick dog might even win a trophy!*

AUTHOR BIO

Diana G. Gallagher lives in Florida with three dogs, eight cats, and a cranky parrot. She has written more than 90 books. When she's not writing, Gallagher likes gardening, garage sales, and spending time with her grandchildren.

ILLUSTRATOR BIO

Adriana Isabel Juárez Puglisi has been a freelance illustrator and writer for more than twenty years and loves telling stories. She currently lives in Granada, Spain, with her husband, son, daughter, two dogs, a little bird, and several fish.

Glossary

annual (AN-yoo-uhl) — happening once every year or over a period of one year

customers (KUHSS-tuh-murz) — the people who buy things from a store

exhausted (eg-ZAWS-tid) — extremely tired

gloomy (GLOO-mee) — dull and dark

loyal (LOI-uhl) — firm in supporting or faithful to one's country, family, friends, or beliefs

quirk (KWERK) — a peculiar trait or strange way of acting

spectators (SPEK-tay-turz) — people who watch an event but do not participate

Discussion Questions

1. What are some other ways Mr. J could have saved his pet store? Talk about some different solutions.

2. What is the best trick your pet knows? If you don't have a pet, talk about an imaginary trick you would teach your pet.

3. What are some other categories that could have been in the Pet Haven Pet Show? Talk about some possibilities.

Writing Prompts

1. Imagine you are a judge at the Pet Haven Pet Show. Write a paragraph about which pet you would have awarded Best in Show and why.

2. What do you think a flyer for the pet show would look like? Draw one and make sure to include all the necessary information.

3. What do you think the best part of having a pet is? What is the hardest part? Write a paragraph about each.

Choosing the Right Pet for You

Having a pet is a lot of fun, but it's important to remember that choosing a pet is also a big commitment. Your pet will be with you for a long time, so it's important to think things through before bringing a new animal home. Here are some questions to consider when choosing a pet.

- How big will the pet grow to be?

- How much care and attention will the pet need? Who is going to be taking care of it?

- Do you have enough room for a pet? Remember that your home is also your pet's home; it will need room to play and exercise.

- Is anyone in your family allergic? If so, you should consider a hypoallergenic pet.

Doing your research ahead of time will make finding the perfect pet an easy process and help ensure you and your pet are happy together. Once you've answered these questions, read up on different types of animals and breeds. You should also talk to a vet ahead of time to figure out which pet is perfect for you.

Pet Friends Forever

READ THE WHOLE SERIES
and learn more about
Kyle and Mia's animal adventures!

Find them all at
www.capstonepub.com

Pet & Friends Forever
A No-Sneeze Pet

by Diana G. Gallagher

Pet & Friends Forever
The Great Kitten Challenge

by Diana G. Gallagher

Pet & Friends Forever
Mice Capades

by Diana G. Gallagher

Pet & Friends Forever
The Doggone Dog

by Diana G. Gallagher

Pet & Friends Forever
Problem Pup

by Diana G. Gallagher

Pet & Friends Forever
The Pet Store Pet Show

by Diana G. Gallagher

THE FUN DOESN'T STOP HERE!

Discover more at www.capstonekids.com

Videos & Contests
Games & Puzzles
Friends & Favorites
Authors & Illustrators

Find cool websites and more books like this one at **www.facthound.com**. Just type in the **Book ID:** 9781479521777 and you're ready to go!